S0-BIA-808

DISCARDED
Bruce County Public Library
1243 MacKenzie Rd.
Port Elgin ON N0H 2C6

I Wish I Had Glasses Like Rosa

Written by Kathryn Heling and Deborah Hembrook
Illustrated by Bonnie Adamson

To all my little kindergarten friends with glasses, especially Kat
⌒ *Mrs. Hembrook*

To Joshua and Amy, best friends
⌒ *Kathryn Heling*

To Jenny and Steffie always, glasses or not
⌒ *Bonnie Adamson*

Text © 2009 Kathryn Heling and Deborah Hembrook
Illustration © 2009 Bonnie Adamson

All rights reserved. For information about permission to reproduce selections from this book, write to:
Permissions, Raven Tree Press, a Division of Delta Systems Co., Inc., 1400 Miller Parkway, McHenry IL 60050.
www.raventreepress.com

Heling, Kathryn and Hembrook, Deborah.

    I Wish I Had Glasses Like Rosa/written by Kathryn Heling and Deborah Hembrook;
    illustrated by Bonnie Adamson;—1st ed.—McHenry, IL: Raven Tree Press, 2009.

    p. ; cm.

    SUMMARY: Abby goes to elaborate and comical lengths to get glasses like Rosa.
          She realizes she might have something that is just as desirable as the
          longed-for glasses. Abby gains appreciation of her own uniqueness.

English–Only Edition
ISBN: 978-1-934960-48-6 Hardcover
ISBN: 978-1-934960-49-3 Paperback

Bilingual Edition
ISBN: 978-0-9724973-7-4 Hardcover
ISBN: 978-0-9770906-5-5 Paperback

    Audience: pre-K to 3rd grade
    Title available in English-only or bilingual English-Spanish editions

    1. Eyeglasses--Juvenile Fiction. 2. Individuality--Juvenile Fiction. 3. Self-Esteem--Juvenile Fiction.
    I. Heling, Kathryn and Hembrook, Deborah. II. Adamson, Bonnie, ill. III. Title. IV. Series.

Library of Congress Control Number: 2009921098

Printed in Taiwan
10 9 8 7 6 5 4 3 2 1
First Edition

Free activities for this book are available at www.raventreepress.com.

I Wish I Had Glasses Like Rosa

Written by Kathryn Heling and Deborah Hembrook
Illustrated by Bonnie Adamson

Raven Tree Press
A Division of Delta Systems Co., Inc.
www.raventreepress.com

Hi, my name is Abby.
This is my best friend, Rosa.
I wish I had glasses like Rosa.
They make her look beautiful!

4

Rosa and I like to build.
We wear safety glasses.
I love wearing glasses!

One morning, I wore my grandma's reading glasses.
Everything looked funny.

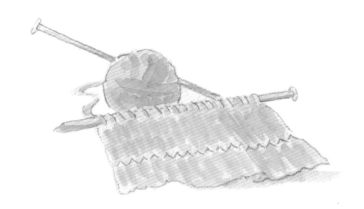

10

Then they slipped off my nose.
I'll never do THAT again!

When I swim, I wear goggles.
I pretend they're real glasses.

14

I wear them on the beach, too.

16

In art class, I made glasses out of clay.
They were perfect.

Then they drooped.
I'll never do THAT again!

19

I found the glasses my dad wore for a party.

They made my nose itch.
Dad said I needed a shave.

23

At recess, I wore my eyeball glasses.

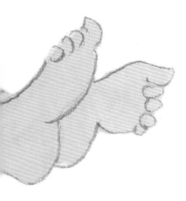

The eyeballs bounced when I jumped rope.
I'll never do THAT again!

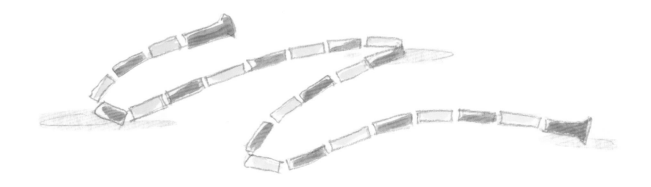

27

I still wish I had glasses like Rosa.
But Rosa wishes SHE had
freckles like me!

28

Imagine that!

32

Bruce County Public Library
1243 Mackenzie Rd.
Port Elgin ON N0H 2C6